SUPER SAMMY GOES TO SCHOOL
A Positive Tale About Type 1 Diabetes
Copyright © 2022 by Josh Hall (Gilda Books)

All rights reserved. No part of this book may be used or reproduced in any manner whatsoever without written permission except in the case of brief quotations embodied in critical articles or reviews.

For information contact:
Josh Hall at jdj.hall@gmail.com

ISBN: 978-0-473-62292-3 (Softcover),
978-0-473-62293-0 (Epub), 978-0-473-62294-7 (Kindle)
First Edition: March 2022

For all children with Type 1 Diabetes

One sunny Monday morning,
Chase woke up in his bed.
The holidays were finished,
And school was now ahead.

Chase was very excited,
Boy, he was feeling great!
Because today at school he'd see,
Sammy, his best mate.

Sammy and Chase did *lots* together,
They'd hang out everyday.

Lately Sammy had been unwell, Chase hoped his friend was okay.

When the bus arrived at school, Chase started walking to class.

He heard a whistle and spun around,
Sammy was there on the grass!

Chase was surprised to see Sammy,
Who looked so *healthy* and *strong*.
"I heard that you were sick," he said.
"May I ask you what was wrong?"

"I was feeling quite unwell," said Sammy.
"So to the nurse I went.
I have *Type 1 Diabetes*..."

...Chase wondered what this meant.

"It means my body needs some help,
So I make sure it's okay.
I need to check my *blood sugar*,
And take *insulin* each day."

This all sounded quite scary,
And Chase began wondering whether,
They could still do all the wonderful things,
They loved to do together.

"Of course we can!" said Sammy.
"As long as I'm aware,
To notice how I'm feeling
And make sure I take care."

"I may begin feeling *icky*,
Grumpy or *sleepy* too.
If I do, I check my blood,
To see what I need to do."

"Well done, Sammy!"

"Can you still play sports?" asked Chase.
"Yes, the doctor said so!
I just need to check my blood sugar,
So it doesn't go too high or low."

"GOOOOAL!!!"

"What about eating food?" asked Chase.
"Can you still eat lunch?"

"As long as I have the right insulin,
Then I am free to MUNCH!"

"What about the playground?
Will you still be okay?"
"You bet I will!" said Sammy.
"Now come on, let's go *play!*"

"WOOHOO!!!"

"What about swimming in the pool?
Is that something you can do?"
"Of course I can!" said Sammy,
"Now look out, *coming through!*"

"CANON BALL!!!"

"What a really fun day!" said Chase.
"And thanks for helping me see..."

"Diabetes hasn't changed you,
You're still the same as me!"

ABOUT THE AUTHOR

My name is Josh and I also have Type 1 Diabetes.

This book is dedicated to ALL children who live with diabetes - no matter who they are or where they are from.

If you enjoyed this book, please consider leaving a review on Amazon.

Thanks for reading!
Josh

CHECK OUT THE FIRST BOOK!

Sammy is an awesome kid who loves playing as a superhero with their loyal pet dog, Scout.

But one day Sammy starts to feel a bit *strange*... and before long is taken to hospital and diagnosed with Type 1 Diabetes.

Confused and frightened, Sammy has a lot of questions. Does this mean the days of being a superhero are over?

Super Sammy is a heartwarming tale that shows children that life goes on after being diagnosed - and although some things change, the important things don't need to.

AVAILABLE ON AMAZON

Made in the USA
Columbia, SC
18 May 2022